## Praise for *Too Much Space!*

"Pretty sporky, as Bob would approvingly put it."
—*Booklist*

"A strong addition to any library's chapter book selection.
Offer to kids who love funny stories but may be too
young for books like *Diary of a Wimpy Kid*."
—*School Library Journal*

# Double Trouble

Read all about Beep and Bob's adventures in space!

## Double Trouble

written and illustrated by Jonathan Roth

ALADDIN

New York London Toronto Sydney New Delhi

JУ
ROTH, J.

This book is a work of fiction. Any references to historical events, real people, or real places are used fictitiously. Other names, characters, places, and events are products of the author's imagination, and any resemblance to actual events or places or persons, living or dead, is entirely coincidental.

**ALADDIN**
An imprint of Simon & Schuster Children's Publishing Division
1230 Avenue of the Americas, New York, New York 10020
First Aladdin hardcover edition December 2018
Copyright © 2018 by Jonathan Roth
Also available in an Aladdin paperback edition.
All rights reserved, including the right of reproduction in whole or in part in any form.
ALADDIN and related logo are registered trademarks of Simon & Schuster, Inc.
For information about special discounts for bulk purchases, please contact
Simon & Schuster Special Sales at 1-866-506-1949 or business@simonandschuster.com.
The Simon & Schuster Speakers Bureau can bring authors to your live event. For more information or to book an event contact the Simon & Schuster Speakers Bureau at 1-866-248-3049 or visit our website at www.simonspeakers.com.
Book designed by Nina Simoneaux
The illustrations for this book were rendered digitally.
The text of this book was set in Adobe Caslon Pro.
Manufactured in the United States of America 1118 FFG
2 4 6 8 10 9 7 5 3 1
Library of Congress Control Number 2018957804
ISBN 978-1-4814-8862-4 (hc)
ISBN 978-1-4814-8861-7 (pbk)
ISBN 978-1-4814-8863-1 (eBook)

*For Gwen and Arthur*

# ★ CONTENTS ★

# Double Trouble

## SPLOG ENTRY #1:
## Hard Work Is Hard!

Dear Kids of the Past,

Hi. My name's Bob and I live and go to school in space. That's right, space. Pretty sporky, huh? I'm the new kid this year at Astro Elementary, the only school in orbit around one of the outer planets. There's just one micro little problem:

GETTING GOOD GRADES HERE IS NEARLY IMPOSSIBLE!

I mean, back on Earth at my old school, I got a trophy for learning how to Velcro my shoe. But if you dare ask the teachers here for a little help putting on your space helmet the right way so your head doesn't explode, they deduct six points from your grade average and make you sharpen pencils for a week!

Beep just clapped and said, "Head go pop, yay!" Beep is a young alien who got separated from his 600 siblings when they were playing hide-and-seek in some asteroid field. Then he floated around space for a while, until he ended up here. Sad, huh?

You know what's even sadder? I was the one who found him knocking on our space station's air lock door and let him in. Now he thinks I'm his new mother!

On the bright side Beep not only likes sharpening pencils but also most of the other mind-numbing tasks I give him. Which frees up my time to do more important things like . . . like . . . like . . .

"Bob-mother like sleep late!" Beep said.

Well, who doesn't?

Beep is also really good at drawing, so I let him do all the pictures for these space logs (splogs, as we call them) before sending them back in time for you to read. Beep says to tell you that he once was terrible at drawing, but that he worked really hard and that you can too. (Unlike me, of course, who was smart enough to give up art the second I realized I could draw only stick figures!)

Anyway, I promise to try to write more entries soon, maybe between my after-school nap and my predinner rest time.

Enjoy!

## SPLOG ENTRY #2:
## Sad and Sadder

Okay, so things didn't go exactly as planned. Somehow, I accidentally napped through dinner, and then I accidentally played video games for four hours, and now it's past midnight and I still haven't started my giant homework project that was assigned only two weeks ago and is suddenly due tomorrow.

Beep patted his tummy as he floated across the

dorm room we share. (Sadly there's no gravity in space.)

"Din-din yummy tonight," he said. "Beep eat for Beep, and Beep eat for Bob-mother, too."

"Why didn't you wake me?"

"Bob-mother look cute when drool on pillow."

No one had ever called me "cute" before. But that was beside the point. "Listen, Beep, we have to focus on this project. Are you going to help me or what?"

Beep clapped. "Or what!"

"Help me look for the work sheet with the assignment written on it." I opened a drawer, and a bunch of papers and junk floated out.

"This work sheet?" Beep said, holding up a floppy manila time-velope.

"No, that's for mailing our splog journals to the kids of the past."

Beep studied the time-velope. "Mail Beep and Bob-mother to past too?"

"We'd have to be two inches tall, Beep, to fit in there. Besides, those aren't meant for mailing people."

Beep shoved the time-velope in his pouch. "This work sheet?" he said, holding up a crumpled paper.

"That's the one!" I grabbed it from him and read. "All we have to do is build an accurate model of a famous structure, such as the Eiffel Space Tower, using ice pop sticks."

Beep clapped again. "Ice pop sticks, yay!" Ice pops were kind of Beep's weakness.

"The best model in the class will be chosen to represent our school at the Ice Pop Stick Finals on Earth's moon. Which, you know, actually sounds kind of fun. I've never been to the moon."

"Beep neither."

I lowered the paper. "I've also never won anything. I wonder what that's like, to win a contest in front of everyone. With all the kids and teachers gazing up at you and everything. It must be the best feeling ever."

Beep clapped. "Bob-mother win prize! Go to moon!"

"Well, not *yet*. But I suppose there's a chance. If we work really hard."

"Bob-mother no like work hard."

"That is a problem." I straightened with resolve. "But you know what, Beep? We're going to do this project thing, and we're going to do it well. Okay, first we need about ten thousand ice pop sticks."

Beep raised his hand. "Oo, oo! Job for Beep! Job for Beep!" He spun. "Where ten thousand ice pop for Beep eat?"

"Sorry, Beep, that's not how it's done. Professor Zoome gave me *one* ice pop stick"—I reached into my backpack—"and this duplicator ray."

"Ray not look yummy."

"That's because it's a tool, not a treat. Watch." I

let the ice pop stick float, aimed the duplicator, and pushed the button. A yellow ray zapped out. Suddenly, there were two floating sticks.

"See, Beep. Now we just have to do it"—I tried to subtract two from ten thousand in my head—"about ninety thousand and eight something more times." (I'm not so great at math.)

Beep folded his arms. "Beep like eat ice pop better."

"Well, we don't have ten thousand ice pops. So this will have to do." I handed the ray to Beep. "Here, you work on that while I start gluing the sticks together."

Beep immediately pointed the ray at my head. "Idea more better! Make two Bobs. Then work go two time fast!"

"No, Beep, wait—"

He pushed the button. *Click*.

Beep pouted. "No work."

"That's what I was trying to tell you. Duplicator rays are designed to work on objects only. Not life-forms."

"Bob life-form?"

"Yes, I'm a life-form!"

Beep pointed the ray at my desk. "Desk life-form?"

"No, but—"

*Zap!* Suddenly, there were two desks.

He pointed at the dresser. "That life-form?"

"Beep, we don't need another—"

*Zap!*

"Pillow life-form?" Beep said.

*Zap! Zap! Zap!*

"Stop that, Beep! This room is crowded enough!"

"Beep life-form?" He pointed at his foot.

*Click.*

His face grew sad when it didn't work. "But Beep want more Beeps."

"Sorry, Beep, that's not how it works."

He unscrewed a panel on the back of the duplicator ray, exposing the wiring inside. "Beep have idea! Beep switch blue and red wire!"

I shot forward. "Beep, stop fiddling with that! You don't know how it works."

Beep put the panel back on. "Now Beep make ray work on life-form!"

"Give me that!" I said. But as I yanked it away, my finger may have brushed the button . . . just as the ray was pointed at Beep!

*Zap!*

"Oh no!" I froze. "What have I done?"

Beep looked down at himself and pouted. "Ray still not work on life-form. Beep sad."

Next to him, another Beep nodded. "Beep Two *sadder.*"

"Here tissue," the first Beep said, turning.

The second Beep dabbed his eyes.

And I promptly passed out.

## SPLOG ENTRY #3:
## Trouble Times Two

My eyes opened to the sight of Beep patting a wet cloth on my forehead.

"Thanks, Beep," I said. "For a second there I thought you had—"

A second Beep patted me with another wet cloth.

"Gaaahhhhh!" I said. "Beep, what have you done?!"

They looked at each other. Then the truth finally

hit them, and the two Beeps squealed, high-fived, and hugged.

"Guys, keep it down!" I said just as there was a knock on my dorm room door. It was followed by a voice: "Bob, are you okay in there?"

I pointed to the bunk bed. "Quick," I whispered to the Beeps. "Hide!"

Beep took his normal spot on top while, annoyingly, the duplicate Beep took *my* bed.

I opened the door a crack. "Oh, Lani, hey," I said.

Laniakea Supercluster is my best human friend at Astro Elementary. She's smart, cool, and fun, so I do my best to also act smart, cool, and fun whenever she's around. (The key word there is "act.")

"What's going on?" she said. "I was passing by and heard all this commotion."

"Oh, that was just Beep making some noise," I said. "And me. And Beep. I mean, Beep making more noise. *Not* a second Beep."

She gave me a funny look.

"So," I said, trying to change the subject, "what are you doing up so late?"

"Homework," she said.

"Me too!" I admitted. "After all, our ice pop stick thingies are due in just a few hours."

"Not *that* assignment, Bob. I finished that ages ago. I'm studying for my final exams for eighth grade."

"Eighth grade! But that's"—I counted on my fingers—"sixteen years from now!"

She laughed. "Not quite."

Beep and Beep giggled from the bed. I tried to talk loudly so she wouldn't hear them. "Speaking of science," I said, "I was wondering: What would happen if someone, uh, switched the red and blue wires on a duplicator ray, and accidentally zapped their little buddy?"

Lani thought. "Theoretically, switching the wires could allow for animate organic matter, or *life-forms*, to be duplicated too. But as I said, only theoretically."

★ 17 ★

The Beeps giggled again.

"So if someone *theoretically* duplicated someone," I went on, "it would be pretty easy to reverse, right?"

She pinched her chin. "As far as I know, the

creation of matter cannot be reversed without risking total annihilation of the universe. Why do you ask?"

I gulped. "No reason. Well, nice talking to you. Good night!"

I felt bad about closing the door on her, but I was in a near panic. I shot around the room. "Quick, Beep, I'll throw away the duplicator ray, and you get rid of the extra Beep."

The other Beep floated out from the sheets. "Get rid of Beep Two make Beep Two sad." He flashed those big Beep eyes.

"Listen," I said, "I'm really sorry, but . . . would you stop looking at me like that?!"

"Bob-mother mean," Beep said.

Beep Two nodded. "We need new Bob-mother," he said, and promptly grabbed the duplicator from my hands.

I lunged forward. "NO, WAIT, I—"

*Zap!* A yellow flash blinded me. Then all I saw were blinking spots. But as those faded, a face came into focus. A face that looked exactly like mine.

"Hello, Bob," the other Bob said.

"Oh, hey," I answered back. And once again passed out.

## SPLOG ENTRY #4:
## Backward Bob

When I opened my eyes again, I tried not to freak out at the sight of the other me who was staring right back.

"This. Is. Weird," I said.

"Rather," the other Bob replied.

I studied him for a moment. "Do I really look like that?" I asked.

Beep Two shook his head. "No, new Bob-mother more handsome."

Original Beep nodded. "More handsome much!"

"But we're the same!" I said.

"Not *same* same," Beep said. "He backward."

I studied him closely. "He doesn't look backward to me. It's like staring into a mirror."

My reflection folded his arms. "Exactly. And reflections are *flipped*." He grabbed the duplicator from Beep Two. "It appears someone switched the red and blue wires, reversing the polarity, which not only reverses the life duplication settings, but it also *reverses* what it duplicates."

"And make backward Beep and Bob-mother!" Beep said.

"Backward or not," I said, "mistakes were made, and we have to focus on a way to *un*make them."

"Throw old Bob-mother out space station door?" Beep Two offered.

Original Beep nodded. "May be only way."

"Whoa, wait!" I said. "Let's not be hasty. In fact, maybe there's a positive side to all this."

Backward Bob lifted an eyebrow. "Such as?"

"Like"—I thought for a second—"Beep and I can sleep in and play video games while the new Beep and Bob go to class."

Beep clapped. "Idea good!"

"And every night when we have to do homework," I went on, "our duplicates can do it for us!"

Beep clapped again. "Idea *super* good!"

"And when we get assigned to go on a hazardous space mission . . ."

"All right, we get the point," Backward Bob said. "It's a deal."

I blinked in surprise. "It is?"

"Why ever not?" he said. "After all, you gave us life. Helping you out is the least we can do. I am you, right?" His eyes glinted, and he arched an eyebrow.

"If you really insist," I said, "you and Beep Two

can make our ice pop stick model while we sleep. It doesn't have to be perfect, just best in the class and then better than anyone's at the finals. Got it? Thanks!" I stretched and yawned. "Nice meeting you, backward me. See you in the morning!"

I put my head on my pillow, and in a second I was out.

I woke with a start, not knowing if it was day or night (a problem with living in space), so I rubbed my bleary eyes until the clock came into focus. When I saw the time, I sprang up.

"Beep, why didn't you wake me?!"

"Bob-mother look cute when drool on pillow *again*."

Could I help it if I was so cute? I shot out of bed. "Quick! We're going to be late for class!"

"But Backward Bob-mother already go."

I froze. "So that wasn't a dream? There really is another me?"

"And Beep!"

"Hmm," I said, "this could be a pretty sporky turn of events. You know what this means?"

"Seem good now but then get worse and then end very, very bad?"

"It means, Beep, that for the first time all school year, we're going to have a nice, leisurely breakfast."

Beep clapped. "Strawberry waffle time, yay!"

And, without rushing for once, we were off.

## SPLOG ENTRY #5:
## Space Jam

About a half hour later Beep and I patted our bellies.

"Breakfast is actually good, Beep, when you don't shove it down in ten seconds."

"Beep shove for thirty minute!" He belched strawberry jam.

I stretched my arms. "So what should we do now, Beep? Morning nap? Or video games? Or . . . or . . ." I tried to think of a third option but came up blank.

"Beep miss class. Beep want go say hi."

"I don't know if that's such a good idea. Don't want to interrupt our doubles, you know."

"What if just look?"

I thought about it. "No harm in spying, I suppose," I said. "Okay, let's do it."

We floated from the cafeteria to our classroom. As we arrived outside the door, I heard Professor Zoome saying, "Very good, Bob! Very good indeed!" followed by lots of clapping.

I peeked inside. Everyone was gathered around a giant ice pop stick model of the Eiffel Space Tower.

"It's beautiful, Bob," Lani was saying. "But how did you get all those colorful little blinking lights inside?"

"It wasn't all me," Backward Bob said. "I used this Temporary Shrink Ray to reduce Beep to a one-inch height, and he ran strands of decorative lighting from bottom to top. He also installed a working elevator and a replica of the actual Eiffel Space Tower gift shop, complete with tiny overpriced T-shirts."

"Very good, Beep!" Professor Zoome said.

"But late last night you'd barely even started," Lani said to Backward Bob. "How did you complete it so fast?"

"That's true," Backward Bob said, "which is why Beep and I decided to stay up all night and even skipped breakfast. Great work demands great effort."

Lani looked a bit suspicious, but everyone else clapped. *Oh, please.*

"Not only do you earn a stellar grade, Bob," Professor Zoome said, "but due to the results of the Clap-O-Meter, it is clear that your model will represent our school at the Ice Pop Stick Finals this evening on Earth's moon. And I believe you have a very good chance of winning the coveted Platinum Ribbon and trophy! We will make a class trip of it later this afternoon."

I turned to Beep. "Did you hear that?" I whispered. "He's getting all the credit!"

"Backward Bob-mother did do all work."

"Yeah, but . . . but . . ." It still didn't seem fair. I cleared my throat and entered the room. "A-ahem."

Everyone spun and gasped.

"Oh no," Lani's friend Zenith said. "Not *two* of them."

Professor Zoome folded her arms. "Can someone please tell me what's going on?"

"Uh, just a little duplication incident," I explained. "What can you do?"

"Yes, what can you do, Bob"—Professor Zoome turned—"and Bob?"

"Actually, from now on," I said, "you should probably just refer to me as 'Bob' or 'Bob Prime,' and call that one 'Backward Bob.' This all goes into my splog, and I really don't want to confuse my readers."

"I'm sure they are plenty confused already," Professor Zoome said.

I patted Backward Bob on the back. "Anyway, thanks for finishing my tower in time for the big competition. I can take over from here." I eyed the Eiffel Space Tower model and smiled.

"Hey, you can't take credit for that," Zenith said. "The *other* Beep and Bob are the ones who made it."

"Yeah," I explained, "but Beep and I made *them*."

"And *I* made the classroom rules," Professor Zoome said, pointing to a poster on the wall.

I gulped. "Did I mention it was kind of an accident?"

Rule #1:
NO Duplication
of LIFE-FORMS
ALLOWED

She    pointed   again.

I slumped. "So now what?"

"Now, Bob," she said, "you will be marked tardy and you will take your seat.

Rule #2:
Even if Duplication
is ACCIDENTAL,
work done by
DUPLICATE counts
toward *their*
grade, not
YOURS !!

Only you have no seat, since it is currently occupied by your double, so you will have to jam into one space together."

Beep clapped. "Jam, yay! Beep like strawberry."

Beep Two clapped. "Beep Two, too!"

I hung my head and mumbled, "Could this morning get any worse?"

"And once you are seated," Professor Zoome said, "please clear your desk for a pop math quiz."

And there was my answer.

## SPLOG ENTRY #6:
## Bad Breaking

n case you're wondering, it's pretty awkward having to share a desk with yourself. Especially if you're a chair hog.

I raised my hand. "Professor Zoome? Backward Bob is pushing me off my seat!"

"My pardons," Backward Bob said. "But I was only doing so because he keeps trying to copy my answers." He shot me an evil glare.

Professor Zoome gasped. "Bob, I am very disap-
pointed you would cheat off another student."

"But he's not another student. He's me!"

"No, Bob," she said, "he is your *reverse*. You are impulsive; he exercises self-control. You rush through work; he takes his time. Your hair gets poofier on your right side; his gets poofier on his left."

"Poofier?" I said.

"Moving along," Professor Zoome said, "in light of today's *incident*, we will review objects in nature that come in doubles. Can anyone give me an example?"

Lani raised her hand. "A double star. Which is when two stars are near each other, forming one system." She smiled. "You get two sunsets. Now *that's* pretty."

Zenith raised her hand. "Double helix. Which is the name of a twisting molecular shape that forms things like DNA."

"Excellent," Professor Zoome said. "Any more?"

Beep raised his hand. "Ooh, ooh! Double ice

cream scoop! Beep love double ice cream scoop!"

Professor Zoome sighed. "Obviously, this lesson is at an end. Please line up for music class, and don't forget to bring your transdimensional flutes."

Well, surprise, surprise, Backward Bob turned out to be a better flute player than I am, a better science student, *and* a better cometball player. He was even better at lunch—he picked healthier foods and chewed his food longer!

By the time we had to leave for the moon (to cheer him on for his *awesome, amazing project*), I was pretty much not in the mood.

"Class," Professor Zoome said, "please proceed to the Astrobus docking bay. Blastoff is in ten minutes."

I eyed Backward Bob, who was struggling to get his Eiffel Space Tower model through the Astrobus door. "Spin it left," he said to Beep Two. "No, other left!"

Spotting my opportunity, I quickly floated over. "Need some help?"

"You can help by floating into a black hole," he said.

Not to be discouraged, I grabbed one of the tower supports near the bottom. "The simplest way to fit it through the door would be to"—I twisted with all my might—"*break it!*"

The class gasped.

"Bob," Professor Zoome said, "what are you doing?"

"Nothing," I said. "I'm just trying to"—I gave the model a chop—"destroy this thing!"

Lani pulled me away.

Blaster the bully pointed. "Ha! He didn't even damage it."

*I didn't?*

Backward Bob folded his arms, and his eyes did that glinting thing again. "Poor, weak Bob."

"Hey, if I'm weak, you are too."

He leaned close and grinned. "I'm you *backward*, remember?"

"I've seen enough!" Professor Zoome said. "Lani, please escort Bob to the office. He won't be joining us on our trip."

"Why do I have to take him?" Lani said.

Professor Zoome smiled. "Because you are trustworthy and responsible."

Lani blushed. "Oh, right. C'mon, Bob, let's go."

"But . . . but . . ."

Lani leaned close. "Don't make it worse. It'll be

okay. At least Beep is sticking by you." She glanced around. "Beep?"

I spied him next to Beep Two. "Beep, get over here!"

I hung my head and let her take me away.

## SPLOG ENTRY #7:
## Deep, Deep, *Deep*

I don't get it, Bob," Lani said after we floated for a minute in silence. "Why were you trying to sabotage Backward Bob's chances of winning a Platinum Ribbon and becoming one of the most famous students in the history of Astro Elementary?"

"Yeah, he is a real moon-rock-head, huh?"

Lani stopped. "You're jealous."

"Why shouldn't I be? He's good at everything! And I'm good at . . . at . . ."

"Yes?"

I slumped. "See, that's just it. I'm not good at anything!"

"Oh, Bob, that can't be true. You're good at, uh, uh, uh . . ."

"See."

"Lunch," she said. "You're good at lunch!"

"But he's better!"

"Bob, life isn't all about the fact that your duplicate—and, okay, everyone else at this school—is better than you at everything. You're forgetting what's most important."

"Breakfast? Because I'm good at that, too."

She looked me in the eyes. "Bob, of everyone I

know, you're the best at simply . . . being good."

"Huh?"

"Think about it," she said. "You were the one to open the air lock door for Beep and rescue him when he was lost. And now you look after him like a big brother."

"Bob-*mother*," Beep corrected.

"And when my pet spider Zilly was floating toward the black hole, it was you who saved her." (You might have to see some of my earlier splog journals to know what she's talking about.) "And when I needed cheering up the other day, you told me all those silly jokes."

"That was my life story."

"Whatever. The point, Bob, is that deep down—"

"Deep, deep, *deep*!" Beep added.

"—you're a really good guy."

A warm feeling rose from my stomach (probably

shouldn't have put so much hot sauce on my waffles).
But no, it wasn't indigestion. It was something else.

"Being good at doing things is nice, Bob," Lani
said. "But being good *to others* is better."

I blushed. "Gee, Lani, thanks."

Beep clapped. "Bob-mother good! Bob-mother
good!"

Lani smiled at me. I smiled at Lani.

And then Lani's smile faded.

"Oh no," she said.

"What?"

Her eyes grew wider. "OH NO!"

"What?!"

"If deep down *you're* very good, then deep down
Backward Bob must be—" She spun. "We have to
stop the Astrobus! NOW!"

And we were off.

## SPLOG ENTRY #8:
## Dancing Pirates?

We shot as fast as we could back to the Astrobus docking bay, and made it just as Backward Bob was carrying his Eiffel Space Tower through the bus door.

"Someone stop him!" Lani called.

But no one heard us because they had already boarded. Backward Bob shot us an evil glare as he turned, blocking the entrance.

"So, I suppose you've figured it out," he said.

"I've figured enough," Lani said. "If deep down Bob is good, then at your backward little core—"

"I'm rotten as a bad apple!" Backward Bob finished. "Yes, you've discovered my true nature. But you may not have guessed my brilliant plan."

"Probably not," Lani said. "Why don't you waste time like all villains by slowly explaining it to us?"

He smirked. "Nice try. But the bus is ready to go, and off to the moon I must be. And what a nice view the moon has of the Earth, that pathetic little planet. All I have to do now is to aim this duplicator ray Earthward"—he held it up—"and I will create a beautiful but horrible backward Earth of my own!"

Lani gasped. "An evil Earth?! But what's to stop it from it taking over Earth Prime?"

Backward Bob raised his arms and cackled.

"With me as its leader? Nothing!! Bwhaaa-ha-haaaaaaaaaaaa!"

Next to him, Beep Two added, "Bwhaaa-ha-yay!"

The bus door slid closed, locking us out. Backward Bob waved through the window. "See ya. Never again!"

The Astrobus engines began to roar.

"Uh-oh, we better get out of here," I said. I yanked Lani and Beep out of the docking bay and closed the door just as the Astrobus blasted out with a fiery whoosh.

Instead of thanking me, Lani put her hands on her hips. "When he was giving that long talk, you were supposed to grab him!"

"How was I supposed to know?"

"I was flashing you the signal behind my back!"

"I thought you had an itch."

Lani sighed. "Either way, now they're gone, and we have to think of a plan of our own."

I thought for a minute. "I've got it! All we need is another duplicator ray, plus a freeze ray, a heat ray, a cupcake ray—in case we get hungry—about two dozen dancing pirates, a sixty-foot-tall android— make that *three* sixty-foot-tall androids—a starship, a ninja mask, a . . ."

Beep clapped. "Plan good!"

"You haven't even heard it all yet. But it's foolproof!" I said. "As long as we can get those two dozen dancing pirates." I slapped my forehead. "But where in the galaxy are we going to get dancing pirates at this hour?"

Beep pouted. "Plan bad."

"Wait, I have another idea!"

Lani had already reopened the docking bay door. "I have a *better* plan," she said, leading us to one of the parked buses. She opened the bus door.

"Quick, get inside," she said.

I stared at her in shock. "Whoa, Lani, I never thought of you as the type who would steal an Astrobus." She had a bad side. How cool!

"What are you talking about?!" she said. "I would never steal a bus! I'm using the interbus communicator to warn Professor Zoome."

"Wait," I said, "does that mean you *don't* have a bad side?"

She rolled her eyes. "Are you going to help me or what?"

Beep sat in the driver's seat and started playing

with the steering wheel. "Beep go vroom, vroom!"

Lani reached for the communicator controls. "Calling the Astrobus headed for Earth's moon. I repeat, calling the Astrobus headed for Earth's moon. Come in."

The speaker returned nothing but static.

"You sure you have the right channel?" I asked.

"Yes! Look, it's the only bus listed in flight right now. They're halfway to Earth already!" She tried again, but still nothing.

"Backward Bob must have switched the channels off," I said. "He's just so evil."

"Beep go after Backward Bob!" Beep said, spinning the steering wheel again.

"Stop playing with that," I said. "You might accidentally turn it on."

"Silly Bob-mother. Wheel no turn bus on." He

reached for a green button. "Green button turn bus on!"

The engines sparked to life.

"Beep, turn that *off*!" Lani yelled.

"Okay, turn," Beep said, spinning the wheel. He hit the accelerator. "Then *off*!"

The Astrobus careened in circles around the docking bay, narrowly missing the walls.

"GAAAAHHHHHHHHHHHHH!" I yelled. I pointed to the bay doors, which had slowly begun to open. "Straighten, Beep! Straighten!"

He sat taller in his seat. "Beep posture bad," he admitted.

"STRAIGHTEN THE *SHIP*!"

Beep yanked at the wheel, and we shot through the narrow gap of the doors . . . right into space.

## SPLOG ENTRY #9:
## Moon Mall Fifty-One

We all exhaled. "That was close," I said.

"Well," Lani said, "looks like we have a new plan. Can you fly this, Beep?"

Beep touched the navigation screen, revealing icons of the planets. "Which one Bob-mother want go to? That one? Or that one? Or *that* one?"

I gazed at the icon of the blue-green planet

I knew so well: my home. "Earth. Take us to the moon of Earth."

Beep did as I said. The ship's computer announced, "Estimated flight time fifteen minutes."

I slumped. "Fifteen minutes. That's like forever!" I studied the control panel. "Can we get any games on this thing?"

Beep shook his head. "No game."

"Movies?"

Beep cried, "No movie, either!"

I began to panic. "What are we possibly going to do for fifteen minutes?!"

"Ahem," Lani said. "We *could* use that time to work out our plan. I still don't understand how dancing pirates fit in."

I shrugged. "I forget. Anyway, when it comes to plans, Beep and I pretty much like to wing it."

Beep flapped.

About fourteen long, boring minutes later, the bus began to slow.

"We're approaching Earth," I said.

The beautiful blue marble grew closer. I pointed at the white moon in its orbit.

"Take us there, Beep."

When he tapped the control panel, a list of the most important moon landing destinations popped up.

"Moon Mall One," Beep read. "Moon Mall Two. Moon Mall Three. Moon Mall Fo—"

"Is there anything other than malls on the moon?" Lani asked.

I scanned down the list. "Moon Mall Forty-Nine. Moon Mall Fifty. Wait, here it is: Moon Educational Auditorium (soon to be Moon Mall Fifty-One). That's it, Beep! Take us there as fast as you can, with only one brief stop at Food Court Eleven!"

"Food court, yay!"

I pictured Backward Bob making an evil duplicate Earth and gritted my teeth.

"On second thought, Beep, we can do the food court *after* we save the planet."

Beep gasped. "Bob-mother sure?"

"Well, maybe if there's a drive-through . . . No, Beep, my decision stands. To the educational auditorium!"

## SPLOG ENTRY #10:
## And the Winner Is . . .

Sadly, it took a while to park. Astrobuses were descending into a giant glass dome from every direction.

"Beep beep!" Beep said to the buses in our way.

"There's a spot." Lani pointed, and Beep swerved the bus into the space and popped open the door.

"Watch your step," Lani said. "There's gravity on the moon, though it's only one sixth of Earth's gravity. So each step is like one big bounce."

I grabbed Beep by the foot. "Did you have to tell him that?"

All around us, kids were bouncing from their buses to the giant building, carrying all sorts of ice pop stick models.

"Look," Lani said, "there's a model of Big Space Ben, and one of the Great Space Sphinx. And it looks like that entire class re-created the stone monoliths of Spacehenge!"

All great space monuments were basically great Earth monuments with the word "space" in them. Probably to keep things simple.

Over all the heads, I spotted a bobbing Eiffel Space Tower. "Look, that must be our class!" We zigzagged through the crowd and caught up just as they were about to enter the auditorium.

Professor Zoome did not look happy to see us. "Bob, I thought I sent you to the office!"

"You did, but . . . but—"

Lani took over. "We came to warn you: Backward Bob has a horrible plan to make an evil, duplicate Earth! You have to stop him!"

Professor Zoome raised an eyebrow toward Backward Bob, who was struggling to get his tower through the auditorium door. *"Him?"*

"He does seem kind of bumbling," Lani admitted, "but that's just an act. He's actually razor sharp, highly motivated, and ruthless—the opposite of *real* Bob."

"I'm good deep down," I pointed out.

"Deep, deep, *deep!*" Beep added.

"And I think, Bob," Professor Zoome said, "that not so deep down you're envious of his success. I'm sorry, but unless he appears to pose an actual threat, the show must go on." She spun to bounce away. "See you inside."

We followed the crowds into the auditorium. Everyone was setting up their models on rows and rows of long tables.

DOUBLE TROUBLE

"What now?" I said.

Lani shrugged. "You heard Professor Zoome. Not much we can do until Backward Bob makes a move. In the meantime, we might as well enjoy ourselves. It's not every day we get to come to such an important educational competition."

"Oh, yay," I mumbled.

Lani stopped to admire a model of the Empire Space Building. "Ooh, I bet this one has a good chance of winning a ribbon."

I caught sight of the Eiffel Space Tower an aisle over. "There he is. Let's sneak up and surprise him!"

"No, wait!" Lani cried.

But I had taken matters into my own hands. I ducked down and approached from behind, and just as he didn't expect it . . .

"BOO!" I yelled, jumping out. "Got you!"

A boy who looked about five years old started to cry. An older girl next to him put her hands on her hips and scowled. "How dare you startle my little brother like that! He worked for weeks on his model, and now you come along to ruin it!"

"I . . . I'm sorry," I said. "I thought he was an evil version of me."

The girl rolled her eyes. "Sure, that's what they all say."

Lani pulled me away. "I was *trying* to tell you: There are dozens of Eiffel Space Towers here."

I reddened. "Let's check somewhere else."

Fortunately, our luck turned. Out of nowhere I caught a whiff of popcorn! I raised my head. "Look, Beep—snack bar! Let's go!"

And we were off!

« * « ✪ » * »

A few minutes later, we were catching popcorn kernels in our mouths and keeping an eye out for Backward Bob.

"Shh," Lani said. "They're about to announce the winners."

The auditorium lights dimmed, and a voice boomed over the loudspeakers: "Welcome to the Ice Pop Stick Finals, brought to you by ICE-E-POPS brand ice pops, the best frozen treats in the galaxy!"

"Oooh," Beep said.

"While all of the entrants are winners in a small sense," the announcer said, "only three are *actually* winners, as chosen by the judges of Planet Pops

Incorporated, makers of the best frozen treats in the galaxy!"

"Ahhh," Beep said.

The announcer continued: "The third place Uranium Ribbon goes to: Stella of Starbright Academy, for her model of the Empire Space Building!"

A spotlight shone on the model and its maker, who was being hugged by all her classmates.

"Told you that one was good," Lani said.

"In second place, a Plutonium Ribbon will be awarded to: Newton of the Lunar Lab School for his model of the Levitating Space Tower of Pisa!"

"Mmm, pizza," Beep said.

"Backward Bob's entry is as good as those," Lani said. "If he wins this thing, then we just have to follow the spotlight and we'll have him."

A loud drumroll sounded, and lights flashed in

all directions. "And now the moment you've all been waiting for: To get your free coupon for ICE-E-POPS brand ice pops, just enter promo code G-O-T P-O-P on our intergalactic website now!"

Everyone cheered and took out their phones.

"Oh," the announcer continued, "and the Platinum Ribbon and special first place trophy goes to Bob of Astro Elementary."

Squeals erupted a couple aisles over.

I pointed. "Let's get him!"

## SPLOG ENTRY #11:
## Ribbon Blues

ani, Beep, and I rushed to the spot where the prizewinning Eiffel Space Tower gleamed in the spotlight. Professor Zoome and all my classmates were whooping and clapping. Lucky Backward Bob. Why couldn't that be me?

I stopped. "Where is he?"

Everyone's clapping slowed. They glanced around,

puzzled. A judge held up a sparkly ribbon. "Where is the winner?" she said.

"No worries, I'm sure he'll be here momentarily," Professor Zoome answered before hissing to the class, "Has anyone seen him?"

"Uh-oh," Lani said. "I have a bad feeling."

"Beep, can you spot him?" I said.

Beep bounced. "No there." He turned and bounced again. "No there." And again. "No there." Another bounce: "There! There!"

"Backward Bob?" Lani gasped.

"Backward Bob-mother *and* Beep Two at snack bar!" Beep added. "And now they leaving with popcorn bag. Rush to exit!"

"Good job, Beep!" Lani said. She grabbed my arm. "Let's go!"

But I didn't move. Lani stopped, puzzled. "What's wrong, Bob? Aren't you coming?"

But I could focus only on the judge, who was tapping her foot in annoyance. "If this Bob of yours doesn't show up soon," she said to Professor Zoome, "we'll be forced to award the prize to someone else."

I took a step in her direction.

"Bob!" Lani called. "If we don't go now, he's going to get away!"

I eyed the Platinum Ribbon. It was so glittery and beautiful. I'd never won anything, let alone the grand prize. And they *had* called for Bob of Astro Elementary.

The judge spotted me. "Ah, you must be Bob. Finally."

Professor Zoome shrugged. "Close enough." The class seemed confused, but they applauded anyway.

The judge leaned toward me and smiled. "In the name of Planet Pops Incorporated, makers of the best frozen treats in the galaxy, I hereby present this award to the most deserving, hardworking student of the year. Congratulations!"

The ribbon seemed to come at me in slow motion, like in those movie scenes where the hero has to make

a very important decision and the audience is left in suspense.

"Sorry, my arthritis is acting up again," the judge said. "In just one more second I'll have this on you. Make sure to smile. This is likely going to be the most special moment of your life."

I could feel the entire auditorium about to erupt in cheers. How amazing was it going to feel?

I swallowed. "Beep helped too, so I really can't take *all* the credit."

I eyed Beep, hoping he was enjoying this as much as I was. But the second he saw me, he looked away. "Beep no say yay."

And that's when I knew what I had to do.

Just as it touched me, I brushed the ribbon away. "Sorry," I said. "But as much as I want this, I don't deserve it. You'll have to give it to someone else while I go stop the evil me!"

The judge rolled her eyes. "I so much preferred judging dog shows."

"C'mon, Lani and Beep!" I said. "Nothing can stop us now."

## SPLOG ENTRY #12:
# Outside the Dome

**W**ell, maybe something could stop us. Like getting to the exit and realizing Backward Bob was long gone.

"This is all my fault," I said, kicking at the ground.

Lani nodded. "Sure is."

Beep nodded. "Sure is."

"Don't know what you were thinking," Lani said.

"Don't know what Bob-mother thinking," Beep said.

"If he ever thinks at all," Lani said.

"If Bob-mother ever—"

"Okay!" I said. "I get it." I kicked at the ground again.

Beep bent over. "Careful, Bob-mother! Almost kick yummy popcorn!" He picked a kernel up and tossed it in his mouth.

"You shouldn't eat off the ground, Beep," I said.

Beep nodded and bent again. "Bob-mother have next one." He tossed another kernel my way.

I watched as it slowly floated down. "Wait, Beep. Are you thinking what I'm thinking?"

Beep clapped. "Strawberry jam world?"

"No, the popcorn." I pointed ahead. "Look, it

makes a trail! Backward Bob must have spilled some as he got away!"

"Kernels smart!" Beep said.

Lani smiled at me. "Bob is smart too. Sorry if we sometimes forget."

"It's okay," I said. "Let's go!"

Lucky for us, eating popcorn while bouncing on the moon made for lots of spills. The trail led around the back of the building.

"Careful," Lani said, "he could be hiding near those Dumpsters."

"The popcorn leads that way, toward the edge of the dome," I said. "But why?"

Lani squinted. "There's an air lock door. He must have gone outside!"

We rushed toward the dome and pressed our faces

against the glass. Sure enough, two figures were leaping up a high hill on the lunar surface, leaving a trail of dusty clouds.

"I don't get it," I said. "Where are they going?"

"Oh no," Lani said. "Once they get to the top of that ridge, they'll have a clear sight of it."

"Of what?" I said, but I had already guessed the answer.

Lani went pale. "Of Earth."

## SPLOG ENTRY #13:
## Lani, Too

I didn't love the thought of going outside the safety of the glass dome into the airless atmosphere of the moon, but we had no choice. Luckily, there were some extra helmets and gloves in the air lock. We suited up quickly and opened the door.

"Once Earth is in view," Lani said, "he'll be able to aim at it with the duplicator ray!"

"If only we'd never started goofing off with that

ray to begin with," I said. "Though that probably would have made my splog entries a lot more boring for my readers."

Beep nodded. "This no boring. This fun!" He leaped extra high. "WHHEEEEEEEEEE!"

Lani and I followed. Each leap brought our feet down into the soft dust, scattering it slowly in big puffs. "This *is* kind of fun," I agreed.

"We better pick up the pace," Lani said. "They're almost there."

Ahead of us, a bright disc began to rise over the crest. A beautiful blue-green world.

"Earth," I mouthed. I hadn't been home since leaving for Astro Elementary at the start of the school year.

Two silhouettes stepped in front of my glowing home world. One of them had the outline of a duplicator ray in his hand.

"No, you can't!" I shouted, scrambling over moon boulders as fast as I could.

Backward Bob looked down at me. "Sorry, Bob, old friend," he said, his voice coming through my helmet radio. He turned and lifted the duplicator ray toward Earth. How could we stop him?

"Think about what you're doing!" Lani called up. "If you push that button, then . . . actually, I forget what's supposed to happen. Maybe if you could explain it all to us again. And be sure to start at the beginning."

"Hey, smart thinking, Lani," I said. "And this time I'll remember to grab him."

"Nice try," Backward Bob called out. "But I'm going to push the button now."

"NOOOO!" I yelled.

"NOOOO!" Lani yelled too.

"WHHEEEEEEEEEE!" Beep yelled, bouncing forward like a rubber missile and hitting Backward Bob's arm with full force.

A yellow ray zapped from the duplicator, but thankfully not at Earth.

"You did it, Beep!" I said.

"Yes, silly little alien," Lani said. "You *did* do it. I thank you much!"

It seemed like a funny thing for Lani to say. I turned to see what was going on.

"Uh, Lani," I said, "why am I seeing two of you?"

"Because," Lani said, eyes wide, "the ray accidentally hit *me*! And now there's an evil me, too!"

"Oop," Beep said.

"Well, hello there," Backward Bob said to Evil Lani. "Interested in ruling a backward world together?"

Evil Lani smiled as she approached him. "Hmm, tempting." Her smile faded. "But not really," she added as she chopped his arm, causing the duplicator ray to spin her way.

"Don't worry," she said as she caught it. "I promise not to do something as pointless as shooting a mere planet."

"Whew," I said.

Evil Lani pivoted, aiming the ray into the sunlight. "Not when I can crown myself the terrible queen of my own double *star*!"

And before anyone could stop her, she pushed the button.

## SPLOG ENTRY #14:
## Shrinking Hopes

Everyone gasped as a yellow ray zapped toward the bright ball of fire in the dark lunar sky.

I squinted, looking near but not directly at the sun. To my relief, there remained only one big star. "Whew, nothing happened," I said.

Evil Lani huffed. "But my aim was true! What a piece of junk," she added, tossing the ray against a boulder, where it split with a crack.

Original Lani raised her arms. "Doesn't anyone get it?! Just as it takes light 8.3 minutes to travel from the sun to the Earth, it will take 8.3 minutes for the duplicator zap, moving at 186,282 miles per second over approximately 93,000,000 miles, to reach the sun!"

"Huh?" I said. Math *really* wasn't my thing.

"It means that very soon we're going to have two suns," Lani said, "and with the gravimetric pull of a double star system, the orbits of all planets will change, and Earth will go spinning into oblivion!"

"Um, one more time," I said.

"WE'RE ALL GOING TO DIE!" Lani yelled.

That I got.

"But I still get to be star queen, right?" Evil Lani said.

Backward Bob shook his head. "Sadly, she's not very bright."

Lani nodded. "She's a backward me, remember."

"This really has gotten way too complicated," I said.

"It's not that complicated, Bob," the real Lani said. "The speed of light is a widely known universal constant. In fact, because stars are so far away, when you look in the night sky you're actually looking back in *time*."

"Cool," I said. "But too bad I can't *go* back in time. Then I'd stop myself from duplicating Beep and starting this whole mess to begin with."

Lani gasped. "Bob, wait. You're a genius!"

"I am?"

"Well, maybe not *genius*," Lani said. "But it's a great plan! All you have to do is shrink yourself and mail yourself back in time just in time to warn yourself not to duplicate yourself!"

"I can do that?"

"Well, theoretically," Lani said. "Though, like all things that have never been tried, it would be extremely dangerous."

I gulped.

Lani sighed. "But it hardly matters, because we would need a time-velope *and* a Temporary Shrink Ray, and where are we going to find those in the few minutes we have left?"

Beep reached in his pouch. "Beep have time-velope!" he said, pulling out the one he'd put in earlier.

"Great! But what about a Temporary Shrink Ray?" Lani said.

Backward Bob, standing by a big moon rock, began to cackle. "Oh, you mean like *this* one?" He then pulled it out of his space belt and pointed it at the rock. *Zap!* The rock shrunk to pebble size. "I've been carrying it around ever since I shrunk Beep Two to work on our ice pop stick project."

"I don't suppose we can borrow it?" I said.

He cackled again. "Not even if you say 'please.' Because now I have a *new* evil plan!"

"Oh yeah?" Lani said. "What is it? And please don't omit any details as you slowly explain your plan."

"Well, first of all," Backward Bob said, "I'm going to shrink Evil Lani, because I'm very unhappy that she chopped my arm. Then I'm going to shrink you, Bob, and have Beep put you in his pouch. Then I'm going to shrink Beep and"—as he went on and on, Lani gestured wildly at me.

"Wait, what does that mean again?" I asked. "You have an itch?"

Lani sighed. "Fine, I'll do this," she said, and with one giant moon leap she swooped down and yanked

★ 89 ★

the Temporary Shrink Ray right out of Backward Bob's hands.

She then bounced over to grab the time-velope from Beep. "Quick, I'll shrink you and Beep and send you back to your room last night."

"But . . . but . . . ," I stammered, not exactly liking the thought of being shrunk *or* sent through time. Before I knew what was happening, a green light flashed, and everything seemed to grow around me.

"GAAAAAAAHHHHHHHHHH!" I cried as Lani's gigantic hand scooped me and Beep up and slid us into the time-velope. She then sealed us into darkness.

Beep clapped. "Tiny Beep and Bob-mother go on ride, yay!"

To: BOB'S ROOM

← 1:00 A.M.

GO

I pushed against the narrow walls. "Not yay, Beep. I'm scared of tight spaces! And why does it smell like old socks in here?"

"Beep use extra time to arrange sock collection."

"This ride better be smooth!" But just as I said it, everything began to spin and spin and spin, and I screamed.

Our journey to the past had begun.

## SPLOG ENTRY #15:
## So Confusing

"WHHHHEEEEEEEEEEEEEEE!"
Beep said as we spun back in time in the dark and cramped time-velope.

"Beep, if we survive this, I'm going to make an important vow."

"Never give up?"

"Never get out of bed!"

I moaned as we twirled and twirled, strange lights blinking and flashing all around.

"Beep think big adventure make Bob-mother grow."

I nodded. "Now that you mention it, having to deal with my bad side has helped me with some personal growth."

"No, Beep mean Bob-mother GROW."

My limbs pressed against the tight inside walls of the time-velope. "It is getting less roomy in here. The shrink ray must be wearing off!"

Beep looked down. "Beep start grow too!"

My head pressed against the inside top of the time-velope, causing my neck to bend. "We have to stop this thing, Beep!"

"But no off button!" Beep, also expanding, pressed into me.

"Stop being such a time-velope hog!" I said. "It's getting too tight! I can't breathe! It's also going faster! And faster! And FASTER!"

"WHHHEEEEEEEEEEEEEEEEEEEE!"

"The sides are starting to split! This is it, Beep, this is—!"

The time-velope burst open, dumping Beep and

me into the middle of . . . our dorm room!

Over by my desk, I saw *me* holding a crumpled piece of paper and saying, "All we have to do is build an accurate model of a famous structure, such as the Eiffel Space Tower, using . . . HEY, WHO ARE YOU?!"

"I'm *you*," I said. "From the future!"

"Cool," Past Me said. "Quick, tell me who wins the next Galactic Series. If I bet the right way, I can be rich!"

"No idea," I said. I yanked the paper from his hand and fed it to the paper shredder. "All I know is that you and Beep can't start your ice pop stick project. And you especially can't use the duplicator ray!"

"You mean this one?" Past Me said, pulling it out.

I grabbed the ray and tossed it in the paper shredder too. Which caused the shredder only to spark and jam, but still.

I turned to Beep. "Beep, we did it! We came to the past and prevented ourselves from duplicating ourselves! Now there's no Beep Two and no Backward Bob and no Evil Lani and everything can get back to normal!"

"Actually," Past Me said, "with you two here, there *are* now two of each of us."

I slapped my forehead. "I can't stand this anymore! Okay, I'll tell you what." I pointed at Past Me. "You're going to temporarily shrink Beep and me and put us in a time-velope. Then you're going to send us back to the future."

"But aren't our duplicates in the future?" Past Me said.

"Well, just send us ahead five minutes or something," I said. "As long as you don't use the duplicator ray, our duplicates won't exist."

"But isn't there another Bob five minutes from now?" Past Me asked.

"No, because *we're* the future us!"

"Wow," Past Me said. "Time travel is so confusing."

"Best not to think too hard about it," I agreed.

"Beep make chart," Beep said, handing me a diagram of our plan.

"Guess it checks out," I said.

And even though it didn't involve dancing pirates, that's what we did.

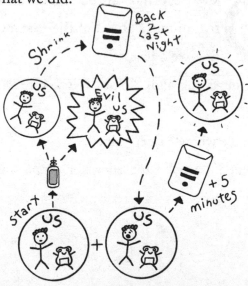

## SPLOG ENTRY #16:
## Making the Grade

Okay, Beep and I are back in our room now, five minutes ahead of the past Beep and Bob we'd just left.

I let out a big sigh. "Now, Beep, it's *really* over. Whew!"

"Double whew!" Beep said.

I smiled. "Maybe too soon for *double* anything, Beep."

Beep clapped.

I suddenly felt my weariness. "All right then," I said with a stretch. "I think we'll sleep well after all the excitement."

Beep picked up the original ice pop stick. "But what about project?"

"I don't think . . . ," I began, but then I remembered how it felt to almost win a ribbon. Maybe, just maybe, I *could* try a little harder.

"Okay, Beep. But this time we're not using any fancy rays. We're doing it the old-fashioned way," I said. "Eating lots of ice pops!"

Beep clapped. "Plan good! Plan *double* good!"

Even with Beep's help, I knew we'd never have enough for a truly award-winning project. But then I remembered something else. I rushed to the door and opened it just as Lani was passing by.

"Oh, hey," I said. "You're up pretty late studying for your eighth-grade finals."

Her eyes widened. "How did you know?"

I shrugged. "Lucky guess."

Beep giggled.

"Anyway," I continued, "I was wondering if you wanted to come in for a little snack? All the ice pops you can eat."

Lani smiled. "Sure, I could use a little break. Sometimes I wonder if I work *too* hard."

Beep giggled again.

And so we stayed up and ate ice pops, and by the time we were done, I had constructed a nice Eiffel Space Tower. It didn't have flashing lights, and it was so small, it fit in my backpack. But I was proud of it anyway.

"You know, deep down," I said, "I think I have

what it takes to get pretty good grades after all."

"Deep, deep, *deep*!" Beep said with a smile, and swallowed the last ice pop whole.

*SEND*

## Bob's Extra-Credit Fun Space Facts! (Even though nothing is fun about space!)

Light is fast. Really fast. Really, really fast. Really, really, *really* fast. Really, re . . . okay, I'm writing "really" too much, but this report is supposed to be 200 words long. And that's a lot of words. I mean, it's really a lot of words. I mean it's really, *really* . . .

Anyway, if you want to get technical, light travels

at 186,282 miles per *second*. So in the time it takes for Beep to say "Yay-one-thousand!" light can go more than halfway from the Earth to the moon, even with a brief stop at the **Intergalactic House of Pancakes**. But even at that super speed, light from the closest star to our sun, **Proxima Centauri**, takes more than four years to get here, and light from the farthest known star, **Icarus**, takes over nine billion!!!!!

Sometime back in all that time long ago is when **dinosaurs** existed, but there are no dinosaurs in space. At least, there better not be. I used to think there were no spiders in space, but sadly I was wrong. I mean, I was really wrong. Really, *really* wrong. Really, *really*, REALLY . . . okay, I'm just about to 200 words. And now Beep is craving strawberry pancakes, so I better go. See ya!

**TURN THE PAGE FOR A LOOK AT**

**BEEP AND BOB'S FIRST ADVENTURE!**

## SPLOG ENTRY #1
## A Horrible Place Called Space

Dear Kids of the Past,

Hi. My name's Bob and I live and go to school in space. That's right, space. Pretty sporky, huh? I'm the new kid this year at Astro Elementary, the only school in orbit around one of the outer planets. There's just one micro little problem:

SPACE IS THE MOST TERRIFYING PLACE EVER!

If you've been to space, you know what I mean: It's dark, cold, airless—and it goes on for infinity! Okay, maybe it ends at some super huge wall. But what's behind that wall? More space? Bigger walls? Giant space *spiders*?!

Just kidding about that last one. There are no spiders in space.

Are there?

No really, are there?

Beep just said to say hi. Beep is a young alien who got separated from his 600 siblings when they

were playing hide-and-seek in some asteroid field. Then he floated around the void for a while, until he ended up here. Sad, huh?

You know what's even sadder? I was the one who found him knocking on our space station's air lock door and let him in. Now he thinks I'm his new mother!

On the bright side, everyone at school says Beep is super cute and fun to have around. And since he won't leave my side, they let him join my class as the school's first alien student. He's definitely a quick learner—he picks up languages in no time, and his grades are already better than mine!

Anyway, I'm writing these space logs (or splogs, as we call them) partly to tell you all about my hectic life, but mostly because it's an assignment to show you how "great" things are here in the future. At the end of each week I'll put all my entries into a time-velope and mail it to 200 years ago. If you receive this, please write back; and while you're at it, please also include a pile of vintage twenty-first-century comic books! Thanks.

Beep will help with the pictures. He's super talented and loves to draw, though in his excitement he sometimes eats all his pencils.

Hope you enjoy!

## SPLOG ENTRY #2
## Space Spiders!

Astro Elementary is a big space station orbiting Saturn. I think they picked Saturn because it looks cool in the brochures.

Trust me, I tried to get out of coming here. When I took the big admissions test, I filled out *C* for every answer. Instant fail, right?

Wrong! Turns out I was the only

kid on the planet this time to get a perfect score. Now everyone thinks I'm some kind of super space genius. I'm a failure even at failing! My parents were more surprised than anything, but as much as I begged, they wouldn't let me stay home *or* send my little sister in my place. She seemed particularly happy to see me go.

Beep and I share a dorm room in the living section of the station. Class starts promptly at 8:00 a.m., so we sleep in until about 7:55, then quickly float through the curved halls to our classroom. (Since there's no gravity in space, we have to float *every*where.)

Professor Zoome is our teacher. She begins each day by taking attendance.

"Zenith?" she called this morning.

"Here," Zenith said.

"Flash?"

"Here."

"Blaster?"

"Here."

(Everyone in my class has pretty cool space names.)

"Bob?"

"Here," I said. (Okay, so not *everyone*.)

When she was done, Professor Zoome clasped her hands together and said, "Class, I have some very good news. After you finish your morning splog entries, we're going on a field trip!"

This time last year, when I was still in school on Earth, we had a field trip where we went on a hayride. I love hayrides!

"To Pluto!" she added.

"Pluto?" I gulped. Pluto didn't have hayrides. It probably didn't even have ponies.